HERE'S HEATHCLIFF by George Gately

AMERICA'S CRAZIEST CAT!

Volume IV

THE BEST OF SUNDAY WITH HEATHCLIFF

HEATHCLIFF

AT HOME

TOR

A TOM DOHERTY ASSOCIATES BOOK

HEATHCLIFF AT HOME

Copyright © 1977, 1978, 1981 by McNaught Syndicate, Inc.

Reprinted by arrangement with Windmill Books, Inc. and Simon and Schuster, a division of Gulf and Western Corp.

First Tor printing: November 1985

A TOR Book

Published by Tom Doherty Associates, Inc
49 West 24 Street
New York, N.Y. 10010

ISBN: 0-812-56818-4
CAN. ED.: 0-812-56811-7

Printed in the United States of America

0 9 8 7 6 5 4

OL' SPIKE NEARLY CAUGHT YOUR CAT THAT TIME, BUT HE GOT STUCK ON A WAD OF BUBBLEGUM!

THE BULLY

by Gately

WE'LL NEVER GET ANY SLEEP!

HEATHCLIFF'S BACK FENCE SINGING IS GETTING OUT OF HAND!

BY THE SEA,
BY THE SEA...

by Geg Gately

AN AFFAIR TO REMEMBER

by Bob Gately

TODAY, BEATRICE AND I MUST HAVE A SERIOUS TALK!

A STYLE
ALL HIS OWN

by Geo Gately

10-9 McNaught Synd., Inc. 1977

... AND NO BITING!

by Bob Gately

WHEN YOU PLAY **MY** TEAM, YOU PLAY **MY** RULES!... NOW LET'S SEE IF YOU CAN GET 'EM STRAIGHT!

OH, WOW! YOU'VE CAPTURED
THE MEANEST GUY IN
THE NEIGHBORHOOD!

FOOTBALL FAN TALES

HE BREAKS ANOTHER TACKLE!...
    HE'S AT THE TEN!....THE FIVE!....
HE GOES IN FOR THE T.D.!!!

OH, OH!...HERE COMES GREAT, BIG LOVABLE CHAUNCY!

CAUGHT
IN THE ACT

by Geo Gately

IT'S THAT SEASON AGAIN

by Bob Gately

1977
12-18 McNaught Synd., Inc.

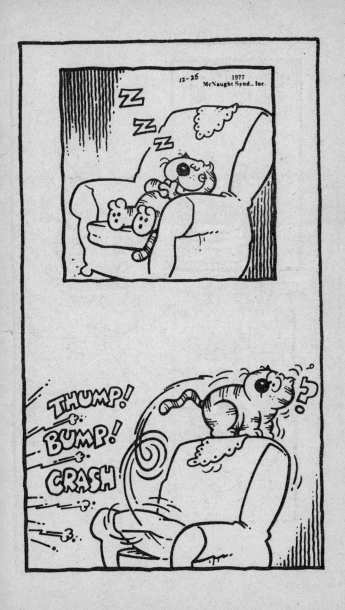

A NAME WORTH GAMBLING ON

by Geo Gately

YOU'VE GOT YOUR NEW COAT ON, SO, STAY OUT OF MISCHIEF!

WHOO, GOSH! MY DOG WAS IN A TERRIBLE FIGHT!...

HE EVEN LOST HIS COAT WITH HIS NAME ON IT!

WHAT'S HIS NAME?

HEATHCLIFF

AMERICA'S CRAZIEST CAT

☐ 56800-1   SPECIALTIES ON THE HOUSE $1.95
    56801-X   Canada $2.50

☐ 56802-8   HEATHCLIFF AT HOME $1.95
    56803-6   Canada $2.50

☐ 56804-4   HEATHCLIFF AND THE $1.95
    56805-2   GOOD LIFE   Canada $2.50

☐ 56806-0   HEATHCLIFF: ONE, TWO, THREE $1.95
    56807-9   AND YOU'RE OUT   Canada $2.50

Buy them at your local bookstore or use this handy coupon:
Clip and mail this page with your order

TOR BOOKS—Reader Service Dept.
49 W. 24 Street, 9th Floor, New York, NY 10010

Please send me the book(s) I have checked above. I am
enclosing $_____ (please add $1.00 to cover postage
and handling). Send check or money order only—
no cash or C.O.D.'s.

Mr./Mrs./Miss _____

Address _____

City _____ State/Zip _____
Please allow six weeks for delivery. Prices subject to
change without notice.